Freddy
AND
Linda

by Jane Quigg

Originally published in 1953

Cover illustration by
Ecaterina Leascencoo and Barbara Cooney
Inside illustrations by Barbara Cooney

Grammar and spelling has been updated.

www.thegoodandthebeautiful.com

CHAPTER 1: THE BOAT RACE

O ne morning at breakfast Mother said, "Freddy, the new house next door has been sold. A family with a six-year-old child is moving in today."

"Good!" said Freddy. "I am glad to hear it. Now I'll have a boy my own age to play with."

"It's a girl," said Mother.

"Oh, I should much rather have a boy," said Freddy. "I wish Johnny Mills had not moved away. I miss him."

"I know you do," said Mother. "I am glad you have invited him to come for a little visit."

"Yes," said Daddy. "We shall all be glad to see him again."

That afternoon when school closed, Mother was waiting for Freddy in the station wagon.

"Have the new neighbors come?" asked Freddy.

"Yes," said Mother. "The girl's name is Linda. I think you will like her."

"Maybe," said Freddy.

Mother smiled at Freddy.

"I think it's a good time to go to the Children's Shop and buy the motorboat you have been wanting," said Mother.

"We had better hurry," said Freddy. "I saw it in the window yesterday, but every day I think it may not be there any longer."

They hurried to the Children's Shop. The little red motorboat was still in the window.

Mother bought it, and they started for home.

When they drove near their house, they saw a girl about Freddy's age standing at the edge of the pond feeding the ducks. A fat little kitten was playing near her.

"I suppose that is the new girl," said Freddy.

"Sure enough," said Mother. "That is Linda." And she waved to her.

When they got out of the car, Freddy

helped Mother carry the groceries into the house. Then he took his motorboat and started toward the pond. Tinker went with him. Tinker was Freddy's dog. He was a black Scotty. He was one year old.

Freddy walked slowly toward the pond.

Tinker went ahead of him and went right up to the new girl and wagged his tail. She bent over and patted him. Then he ran back to Freddy.

When Freddy came up to the new girl, she was feeding the ducks again. She turned around and smiled at him, and said, "Hello, Freddy."

"Hello, Linda," said Freddy.

Linda looked surprised. Then she said, "Did your mother tell you my name?"

"Yes," said Freddy. "And I'll bet she told you mine."

"She did," said Linda. "But she forgot to tell me your dog's name. What is it?"

"Tinker," said Freddy.

"My kitten's name is Mixy," said Linda. "I named her that because her colors are so mixed up. She is a calico cat. And she has double front paws."

Just then Tinker began to growl at the kitten.

"Doesn't Tinker like cats?" asked Linda.

"No," said Freddy. "He chases them."

"Dearie me!" said Linda.

"But he almost never chases kittens," said Freddy.

"Well," said Linda, "when he gets acquainted with Mixy, I know he will like her. I think he will keep on liking her when she is grown up."

"I hope he does," said Freddy.

Linda leaned over and patted the duck nearest her. "These are nice ducks," she said.

"Better be careful," said Freddy. "The edge of the pond is slippery."

"Oh, I won't fall in," said Linda. "My sneakers will keep me from slipping."

"Well, I have warned you," said Freddy.

He wound up the motorboat and put it into the water. Then he and Linda watched it move away. They heard it go z-z-z-z-z.

"I have a sailboat," said Linda. "When I finish feeding the ducks, I will go and get it. Then we can have a race to see whose boat is the fastest."

"I shall be sure to win," said Freddy.

"Motorboats go much faster than sailboats."

"My sailboat sometimes goes quite fast," said Linda.

"But never so fast as a motorboat," said Freddy.

After a while Linda stopped feeding the ducks and went for her sailboat. When she came back with it, she put it into the pond and watched it sail away. Most of the paint was gone, and the sail was torn, but there was a good breeze, and it sailed right along.

"It is a good boat," said Linda, "a very good little boat."

Freddy forgot his manners. "It needs

paint," he said, "and a new sail."

"I know it does," said Linda.

Freddy wound up the motorboat and put it into the pond. Away it went, z-z-z-z-z.

"Let's have the race now," he said.

"All right," said Linda.

"I'll blow my whistle when it is time to start," said Freddy. He took the motorboat from the water and wound it up again.

Linda held the sailboat until Freddy blew the whistle. Then away went the boats.

Z-z-z-z-z went the motorboat.

The sailboat dipped and started away.

Just then a sudden wind caught the

sailboat and made it go very fast. Linda clapped her hands. "Hurry, hurry, little sailboat!" she called.

All of a sudden, the motorboat stopped. It did not say z-z-z-z-z. It said nothing at all.

"Huh!" said Freddy. "Something is the matter with the motor!" He picked up a long stick and gave the motorboat a little push.

Linda's sailboat was on the other side of the pond. The little sailboat had won the race.

"I wanted a motorboat," said Freddy. "But now I wish I had a sailboat."

"It is a good little motorboat," said

Linda. "Are you sure you wound it up tight enough?"

Freddy ran to his yard and brought back a rake and pulled the boat to shore. He turned the key. It clicked and clicked. He wound it up tight. Then he set it in the water. The motorboat was pointed against the wind, but still it went fast, clear to the other side of the pond, and pushed against the shore, still going z-z-z-z-z when it got there.

Freddy said, "I am glad I found that out. After this, I will always wind it up tight."

"My cousin Bob has a toy motorboat," said Linda. "I have often played with it. That is how I knew you must wind yours up tight. I think motorboats are wonderful."

"But a sailboat always works," said Freddy. "Thank you for telling me how to wind my boat. Let's have another race right now."

"All right," said Linda.

They had another race, and this time Freddy's boat won.

Linda and Freddy played until Freddy saw his father drive by. "There goes my father," he said. "It must be time for supper. I shall have to go home now."

"I will go home now, too," said Linda.

They picked up their boats and started off.

As they walked along, Freddy said, "Linda, how old are you?"

"Six and a half," said Linda. "How old are you?"

"Six and a half," said Freddy. "I was wishing a boy my age would move in next door, but I am glad you have come."

"That's funny," said Linda. "I was wishing that twins would live next door to me—twin girls, just my age."

They both laughed.

"I guess we are even," said Freddy.

"What is the name of your school?" asked Linda.

"The Whitman School," said Freddy. "The trees are so close to the windows that sometimes the squirrels come down on the window sills. And we are painting scenery for an autumn play. I have painted a scarecrow."

"Do you like your teacher?" asked Linda.

"Yes," said Freddy. "Miss Coe is friendly. On my first day, she told me she was glad I had come."

"I hope I am put in your room," said Linda.

"You would like it," said Freddy. "We learn a lot, and we have fun."

When they said goodbye, Freddy said, "I'll look for you in school tomorrow morning. There are two rooms for the first grade. I hope you will be in mine. I have invited all the boys and girls in my room and Johnny Mills to a party tomorrow afternoon. Johnny Mills used to be in my room. He lives in Farmington now, but his mother is going to bring him, and he is going to stay all night. Even if you are put in the other first grade room, I want you at my party."

"Thank you," said Linda. "It will be fun."

CHAPTER 2: A PARTY SUPRISE

The next morning Freddy was feeding the ducks at the little pond across the road from his home.

As he fed the ducks, he kept thinking of the fun he was going to have that afternoon at his party.

The ducks were full grown. Freddy knew every one of them. Their names were Mr. and Mrs. McCoy, Frankie, Beatrice, Lulubelle, Dotsy, Dicky, Doris, and Flora. This morning they were all there except Flora.

"Where is Flora?" he said to himself. "She is usually the first one to come to meet me."

Just then Freddy had a big surprise. Flora came out of the little red dollhouse on the other side of the pond and walked proudly to the shore with eleven fluffy baby ducklings in a straight row behind her. She got into the water and swam toward Freddy with her babies following behind, still in a straight line.

The dollhouse was near the outlet of the pond, where it emptied into a narrow channel just above a waterfall.

Freddy could hardly believe his eyes. Flora and her ducklings swam across the pond and up close to the other ducks.

Freddy threw some more pieces of bread into the water. This time Flora and her ducklings picked them up, too.

As soon as Freddy had thrown all the bread to the ducks, he ran to the house for more. When he got there, he told Mother about Flora's family.

"It is very late in the season for baby ducks," said Mother. "They usually come at Easter time. Let's go see them."

Mother hurried back to the pond with Freddy. When they got there, Flora was walking in the path along the side of the pond with her eleven ducklings. When she saw Mother and Freddy, she waddled up to them with the baby ducklings following behind her in a straight line. When she stopped, they all stopped, too, and when she looked up at Freddy, they all looked up, too.

"Good morning, Flora," said Mother. "What a surprise you have given us! And how pretty your babies are!"

After a little while, Mother picked up one of the ducklings and stroked its down. Flora quacked loudly, and all the ducklings quacked, too. Soon Mother put the little duckling down again on the grass.

They fed their bread to the ducks, and then Mother said, "Freddy, isn't it time for school?"

"Almost time," said Freddy, looking at his wrist watch.

Then Mother said, "And, by the way, do you think the boys and girls would like sandwiches and cookies and ginger ale and homemade ice cream for refreshments at your party?"

"Yes!" said Freddy. "Thank you! Please be sure there are enough sandwiches—especially peanut butter ones."

Mother promised to make a good many sandwiches.

They walked back to the yard, and Mother and Freddy got into the car and started for school. As they rode along, Freddy talked about the party. "I won't tell the boys and girls about the baby ducks," he said. "I won't even tell Linda. I think it will be fun to keep Flora's ducklings for a surprise."

"All right," said Mother. "I like surprises."

When they got to the school, Freddy said goodbye to Mother and went in. He was on time. Soon after school began, the principal brought Linda to Freddy's room. Freddy was glad to see her.

Miss Coe found a desk for her and said, "Linda, you have come to our room on a very special day. This afternoon we are going to a party."

"Freddy has told me about the party," said Linda. "I can hardly wait."

All day long in Freddy's room the children thought about the party. They had all brought bread in paper bags to feed the ducks when they got to Freddy's house.

At last it was a quarter to three, and time to leave for the party. Miss Coe and the children started off. They talked and laughed as they walked along. Freddy laughed too, thinking of the surprise Flora's ducklings would be for them at the party.

When they came to a bridge near Freddy's house, they stopped to look at the waterfall.

"See how fast the water comes!" said one of the girls. "Freddy, do the ducks ever swim over the waterfall?"

"No," said Freddy. "They know better. They probably would drown if they tried to do that. But sometimes they swim close to it."

When they got to Freddy's house, Mother and Johnny Mills were in the yard waiting for them. Soon they all went to the duck pond. Mr. and Mrs. McCoy, Frankie, Beatrice, Lulubelle, Dotsy, Dick, and Doris came up on the shore to meet them. When the boys and girls and Miss Coe threw bread into the water, the ducks hurried into the pond and ate it up.

Freddy kept looking for Flora and her ducklings, but they did not appear.

In a little while, Mother said, "Perhaps we had better go back to the yard now."

They went to the yard and sat at two long tables on the terrace and ate

sandwiches and drank ginger ale. Then
they had the ice cream and cookies. And
they all talked and laughed and had a fine
time.

Freddy kept wondering if Flora and her
ducklings would appear in time. Every
little while he asked Mother if they had
come to the pond yet. Mother said she
would go and see. But when she got back,
she told him that they were not in sight.

After the boys and girls had finished
eating, they played games until Miss Coe
said she was afraid they had to go because
it was getting late.

"Let's go and say goodbye to the
ducks," said Alice Evans.

"Yes, let's," said the other boys and

girls.

Freddy hurried on ahead with Johnny Mills and Danny Dixon.

"There they are!" said Danny. "All the ducks are on the shore waiting for us."

"Not all," said Freddy to himself. "I wonder what has happened to Flora and those ducklings of hers."

Miss Coe and the boys and girls stayed a few minutes to watch the ducks. Then they said goodbye to Mother and Freddy, and they were all ready to leave when Freddy called, "Oh, look! Here comes the surprise!"

They all looked and saw Flora and her babies swimming down the stream.

How pleased the boys and girls were! Freddy ran into the house for more bread. The other big ducks came up to get their share. But the boys and girls aimed the pieces of bread toward Flora and her babies.

When Miss Coe and all the children except Freddy, Linda, and Johnny Mills had gone, Mother said, "It was a good party, wasn't it, Freddy?"

"Yes, it was," said Freddy. "But Flora kept me guessing. I was afraid she and her ducklings would not get to my party. I guess I was the one who was surprised after all—when I saw them swimming down the stream!"

"I knew about the baby ducks," said

Linda. "After you had left for school, I went to the pond to say good morning to the ducks, and I saw them then. But I did not tell. I guessed that you were keeping them for a surprise."

CHAPTER 3: FISHING

One Saturday morning Mother woke Freddy at five o'clock. He jumped out of bed and hurried into his play clothes. Today was the day he was going trolling with Uncle Ben. Uncle Ben had told Freddy that trolling was the way to fish for bass. It was drawing your line through the water behind a moving boat. And Freddy had offered to row the boat for him.

Freddy went to the kitchen and had a big breakfast of oranges, oatmeal, bacon, and eggs.

After breakfast Mother and Freddy did the dishes, keeping as quiet as could be so as not to disturb Daddy. He was a doctor and had to be out late the night before. As soon as the dishes had been put away, Mother and Freddy started off.

"I suppose Linda is still asleep," said Freddy. "I wish she was going with us."

"We will take her sometime soon," said Mother. "But right now you and I should be starting out for Uncle Ben's."

Apple Hill Farm, where Uncle Ben lived, was twenty-nine miles out in the country on a hill near a lake. It was Freddy's favorite place to visit.

Uncle Ben was an old man who lived alone. He was not Freddy's real uncle, but

Mother and Daddy and Freddy knew him so well that they called him Uncle Ben. They went to see him often.

Mother and Freddy rode quickly out of the city into the dewy countryside.

They passed by long stretches of roadside where banks of goldenrod and Queen Anne's lace stood tall and beautiful. After a while, they passed some orchards where the trees hung heavy with red apples.

Half an hour later when they drove into Uncle Ben's yard, he was waiting for them. He had the oars and a fishpole and a can of night crawlers.

"This is starting out to be a cloudy

morning," said Mother. "It should be good for fishing."

"Yes," said Uncle Ben. "The fish bite better on a darkish day like this."

"May I carry the fishpole?" Freddy asked. "Are you coming, Mother?"

"I think I would rather stay here, if Uncle Ben would like to have me make an apple pie," said Mother.

"Apple pie sounds good," said Uncle Ben. "With Freddy to help us eat it, I know we shall have good use for it."

"I think Tinker would like to stay with you," said Freddy. "He would not like keeping still in a boat."

Then Uncle Ben and Freddy said

goodbye and started off. They walked down the path under the orchard trees full of ripe red apples with big red-breasted robins among the branches. Then they went across the meadow through the huckleberries toward the lake.

When they got to the dock, they found a big boy there. Uncle Ben knew him. "Good morning, Rick," said Uncle Ben. "You are up early, too."

"Yes," said Rick. "I am going to work on the engine of my motorboat. It looks as though you are going trolling."

"Right you are," said Uncle Ben.

Then Rick said, "I will unfasten your boat and push it off when you are ready."

Uncle Ben thanked Rick. Then he said, "Hop in, Freddy."

Freddy climbed into the boat. Uncle Ben put the oars in the oarlocks for him. Then he took the pole past Freddy to the back of the boat and sat down. He said to Rick, "Shove her off!"

Rick unfastened the boat and gave it a push. Uncle Ben thanked him. Then he looked at Freddy and grinned, and Freddy grinned back. Freddy pulled on the oars, and the boat began to move through the shady coolness near the shore.

Uncle Ben threw out his line with the baited hook at the end, and in a couple of minutes he pulled in a fair-sized fish. Freddy rowed slowly and softly.

All was quiet on the lake. Uncle
Ben caught three perch in less than ten
minutes.

All of a sudden, through the stillness,
they heard a woman calling from a dock
in front of a cottage. "Oh, Uncle Ben!
Please row in closer."

"Miss Pimm seems to need us," said
Uncle Ben.

Freddy quickly rowed up to the dock.
Miss Pimm leaned over and uncovered a
strawberry basket and showed them a tiny
ruby-throated hummingbird in the basket.

"I found him a few weeks ago under my
lilac bush," she said. "His right wing has
been hurt. I took him to a veterinarian,

and he tells me that it will soon be well. In another week the little fellow should be able to fly again. Isn't he pretty?"

Uncle Ben and Freddy thought he was, and said so.

"I have been feeding him honey and water with a medicine dropper," she said, "but there isn't a bit of honey left for his breakfast. Would it be too much trouble to get a jar of honey for me at Mr. Norton's store?"

"Of course not," said Uncle Ben. "It will be a pleasure. We shall soon be back."

They started off. Freddy rowed faster. In a few minutes, Uncle Ben said, "Now in to the shore here."

Freddy pulled in to shore, and Uncle Ben fastened the boat securely to Mr. Norton's dock. Then he and Freddy walked up to Mr. Norton's store.

"Benjamin Baxter," said Mr. Norton, "you are just the man I want to see. I have to be away for an hour or so. I have to deliver a pound of tea to an old lady in Dark Hollow, and I need someone to tend store. I wonder if you would do it for me."

Uncle Ben told Mr. Norton about their errand for Miss Pimm.

"I'll run right over with the honey in my wagon," said Mr. Norton.

When Mr. Norton got back to the store, he showed Freddy how to get down boxes of cereal, washing powder, and other things from the top shelf with a long pole which had a pair of iron tongs at the end of it.

As soon as Mr. Norton had gone, Mrs. Robinson came to buy groceries. "Oh, Uncle Ben," she said, "I was over to your house an hour or so ago, looking for you. I want to ask if you would let me have some of your dahlias to decorate the church for my niece's wedding this evening."

"As many as you like," said Uncle Ben. "I shall be proud to have my flowers at Miss Betsy's wedding."

"Thank you ever so much, Uncle Ben," said Mrs. Robinson. "Whatever should we do without you?"

"Shucks!" said Uncle Ben. "What is a garden for? And what would I do without my neighbors?"

When Uncle Ben had put Mrs. Robinson's order into her market basket, Freddy carried the basket out to her car.

Next Mr. Coleman came into the store. While Uncle Ben waited on him, they talked about fishing, and about the weather, and about who would be the next president.

When Mr. Coleman went out, Freddy said, "Uncle Ben, you know everybody."

"I wish I did," said Uncle Ben. "Folks are nice to know."

After Mr. Coleman was gone, Freddy and Uncle Ben were alone in Mr. Norton's store for a moment. Then Uncle Ben looked out through the door and said, "Here comes Debbie Dodd, Billy Perkins, and Tommy Hall. And right behind them are Mr. and Mrs. Allen Miller."

"It looks as if we are going to have a very busy time," said Freddy.

"Yes, it does," said Uncle Ben. "We will take care of the youngsters first. I have seen children made to wait in some stores while grownups were taken care of. We won't do anything like that in Mr. Norton's store. He wouldn't like it."

"Of course not," said Freddy.

The children knew exactly what they wanted. Billy bought a red, white, and blue top; Tommy bought a yellow net bag full of marbles; and Debbie bought a picture postcard of the lake, to send to her grandmother.

For half an hour after that, Uncle Ben and Freddy were very busy. Freddy liked the work. He especially enjoyed pulling down the boxes from the top shelves with the long pole which had the tongs on the end of it. And he played with Mr. Norton's big black cat.

When Mr. Norton got back, he thanked them and said, "Now you go out on the back porch and have root beer and ginger snaps."

The ice-cold root beer and the ginger snaps were delicious.

After that Uncle Ben and Freddy said goodbye and started for their boat.

When they got to the boat, Uncle Ben said, "Freddy, I'll row now and let you fish."

Freddy went to the back of the boat and sat down and picked up Uncle Ben's pole. As soon as they got out from shore, Freddy tossed out the line and drew it slowly from side to side through the water just as he had seen Uncle Ben do. Almost at once he felt a fierce tug. Then another and another. He began to reel in the line,

and after a few minutes, he landed a good-sized fish.

"It's a bass, and a big one," said Uncle Ben. "We did not catch any bass before. I guess this is all the fish we can use. We had better go home now."

When they got back to Uncle Ben's docks, Freddy helped Uncle Ben fasten the boat. Then they hurried up the hill and through the orchard until they came to the house. As soon as they came into the kitchen, Uncle Ben spied the apple pie on the table.

"My, that pie looks good!" he said. "Fried perch and apple pie will make a fine lunch."

"Shall we eat the bass, too?" asked Freddy.

"I think you should take the bass home," said Uncle Ben. "I believe your father would like it."

"Yes, and I would, too," said Freddy.

"I shall have lunch ready very soon," said Mother.

After they had eaten lunch, they agreed that nothing could have tasted better.

At two o'clock, Mother and Freddy said goodbye to Uncle Ben and drove off toward home. They stopped only once on the way, to buy some grapes at a roadside stand in front of a little white farmhouse.

When they got home, Freddy showed

Daddy the bass.

"That's a fine fish!" said Daddy. "I hope Mother will cook it for supper."

Mother promised.

Freddy laughed and said, "Mother, isn't this the first time you ever cooked fish twice in one day?"

"I would cook fish twice a day and three times on Sunday," said Mother, "if they were as good as this fish. Now go and get washed up while I get things started for supper."

CHAPTER 4:
MISS PIMM'S HUMMINGBIRD

The next morning when Freddy went to play with Linda, he told her about Miss Pimm's hummingbird.

"I'd like to see him," said Linda. "I have never in all my life seen a hummingbird."

"I wish all the children in our room could see him," said Freddy.

"Do you suppose Miss Pimm would lend him to you?" asked Linda.

"She might," said Freddy. "Let's go and

see if my mother will take us to ask Miss Pimm."

Freddy's mother was willing, and that very afternoon they all started off for Miss Pimm's.

When they got there, they all went to the door, and Freddy told Miss Pimm why they had come.

Miss Pimm smiled at Freddy and said, "I shall be glad to lend you the hummingbird. I am about to feed him. Won't you all come in and watch me?"

It was amazing to see how neatly she did it. The little hummingbird sat on a small branch stuck in a flower holder. She held the medicine dipper a little higher than his beak, and the little bird stuck his

long bill into it and sucked up the honey
and water.

When he had finished, Linda
said, "Please sing us a song, little
hummingbird."

"Hummingbirds do not sing," said Miss
Pimm. "When they fly, their wings move
so fast that they make a humming sound.
And they make the humming sound with
their wings as they hold themselves still
in the air in front of a flower that they are
getting honey out of. Before long he will
be able to fly again. Then he will hum
again."

Then she took the little bird on her
finger off his branch and put him in the
strawberry basket and covered it with a

blue scarf and gave the basket to Freddy.
And she put the medicine dropper, the jar
of honey, and the flower holder with the
small branch in it into a bag. "If he has his
own little twig to sit on, he will feel right
at home," she said.

"How often do you feed him?" asked Freddy.

"Five times a day," said Miss Pimm. "He usually wakes up early in the morning. I give him his breakfast then. At ten o'clock I feed him again. He has his lunch at noon time, a little snack at three, and his supper at seven o'clock."

"Do you ever give him anything but honey and water?" asked Freddy.

"Honey and milk now and then, for a change every other day or so," said Miss Pimm.

"I'll try to do everything exactly right," said Freddy. "I want him to enjoy his visit."

"I feel sure he will," said Miss Pimm.

"I am going to help Freddy take care of him," said Linda.

"That's a good girl," said Miss Pimm.

When they got home, Freddy showed the hummingbird to Daddy and told him that he had borrowed the bird from Miss Pimm.

"He is a bright-looking fellow," said Daddy.

"He is little," said Freddy. "But he eats five meals a day. First, he has breakfast, of course. At ten he eats again. He has his lunch at twelve. At three he has another meal, and he has supper at seven."

"He has a good appetite," said Daddy.

"You will be kept busy feeding him."

"It will be fun," said Freddy. "Linda is going to help me take care of him tomorrow."

"Good enough!" said Daddy. "If you need any extra help, let me know."

At bedtime Freddy lifted the hummingbird from the twig and put him into the strawberry basket and covered him over. He put a jar of honey and water and the medicine dropper beside the basket.

Freddy was so tired that he slept through the night without waking up. When he woke up at six o'clock, he uncovered the basket. The bird was awake. He was looking at Freddy with his bright little black eyes.

"Hello, little fellow," said Freddy. "How long have you been awake? Probably you are hungry."

Freddy hurried to feed him. Then he left the bird on the branch and went down to breakfast.

When Freddy had finished breakfast, Daddy offered to take care of the hummingbird while Freddy and his mother went to Sunday school.

Freddy brought the bird and the branch and the flower holder and the scarf and the strawberry basket down to the living room and put them on the table. Then he set the little bird on his favorite twig.

"Daddy," he said, "if he takes a nap, please put him in the basket and cover him over."

Daddy smiled at Freddy. "Don't worry, I'll take good care of him," he said.

When Freddy and his mother got home from church, Daddy told them that the hummingbird had hopped down from his twig and crawled under the scarf and gone to sleep. "He is still there," he said.

"Oh, can he fly?" asked Freddy.

"His wing must be almost well," said Daddy. "He can flutter a little."

Freddy walked over to the table and peeked under the scarf. "Sh!" he said. "He is sound asleep."

In the afternoon, Linda came over, and Freddy let her feed the hummingbird. First, she took him up on one finger and put him on the twig. Then she put his honey and water in the medicine dropper and held it so that he could put his bill into it. Then she called him "Teeny Tiny."

After Teeny Tiny had finished his meal, Freddy carried the twig in the holder out to the terrace and put it on a table. Then he and Linda played badminton. Teeny Tiny sat on his twig watching them. Freddy and Linda got so much interested in the game that they forgot him for a few minutes. But in a little while Freddy looked down to see how he was, and he was down on the table.

"I wish I had seen him fly," said Freddy.

"I hope Teeny Tiny doesn't fly far away," said Linda.

"I think he can fly only a little way," said Freddy.

All afternoon they kept him on the terrace with them. Before Linda left for home, they fed him again. After Linda had gone, Freddy took Teeny Tiny into the house, and when he was putting Teeny Tiny on the table beside his bed, he said to himself, "I think I will give him honey and milk tonight for his last feeding, just for a change."

Early in the morning, Freddy woke up and found Daddy in the room feeding the little bird. "I looked in on my way out," said Daddy. "The hummingbird was wide awake, and so I decided to feed him."

Freddy laughed. "That little bird is always ready to eat," he said.

"Go back to sleep," said Daddy. "It is still only half past six."

A little later Freddy woke up again, and Mother was feeding the bird. "Where did you come from?" he asked.

"I stopped to tuck you in and found our little friend awake," she said. "I thought he must be hungry."

"Daddy fed him, too," said Freddy. "Everybody seems to like to feed Teeny Tiny."

CHAPTER 5:
TEENY TINY GOES TO SCHOOL

After Freddy had eaten a big breakfast, he put the little bird and all of his things into the car. Then he and Mother started off for the school.

Mother carried the jar of honey and water, the medicine dropper, and the branch in the flower holder to Freddy's room. Freddy carried Teeny Tiny in the strawberry basket.

Mother and Freddy went into Freddy's room, and Freddy put the basket down on his desk. Mother put the things she had carried on Freddy's desk, too.

"I have so many errands to do this morning that I think I ought to go right along," she said. "Miss Coe and the other boys and girls will be here soon."

"All right," said Freddy.

In a few minutes, Miss Coe came. She was pleased to see the hummingbird. "What a fine surprise!" she said. "I know we shall all enjoy our tiny visitor."

"Is this the first hummingbird brought in this year?" asked Freddy.

Miss Coe laughed. "It is the first one, all right," she said, "and it is probably the only one that will be brought in. Where did you get him?"

Freddy told her, and she said, "You must tell the boys and girls, too."

Soon the children began coming in. The little bird pleased them, of course.

"Look at his long bill!" said one.

"And his long, pointed wings!" said another.

"What bright eyes!" said a third.

"Did you ever see such small feet?" asked a fourth.

"I like his pretty feathers," said a little girl.

Then someone said, "I hope he will sing to us."

"He doesn't sing," said Freddy.

Then a boy said, "Let's measure him with a ruler and find out how many inches long he is."

Miss Coe got the ruler from her desk and held it beside the little bird to measure him. He was exactly three and a

half inches long.

When all the children had come, Freddy fed the hummingbird. The boys and girls watched the little bird put his long bill into the dropper and suck up the honey and water.

Then Freddy told them about how he had gone trolling with Uncle Ben and met Miss Pimm. They listened to every word. As soon as he stopped talking, Miss Coe and the children began asking him questions. Freddy felt happy as he answered.

During the day, some of the time Teeny Tiny sat in the strawberry basket and some of the time he sat on his twig. His little bright eyes seemed to see everything that was going on. Once he took a short nap, and the boys and girls tiptoed about the room and talked softly until he woke up.

At recess time Freddy took the hummingbird to the playground in the strawberry basket. While the other children played games, he held the basket and watched. In a little while, Susan Smith asked to hold the basket. And then Barbara Horton offered to hold it. And then Donald Barter offered. Before recess was over, seven boys and girls had held Teeny Tiny's basket for Freddy.

After recess, Miss Coe suggested that Freddy take the hummingbird around to all the rooms. "I should like to have all the children see him," she said.

"That's a good idea," said Freddy.

Freddy visited every room in the Whitman School with Teeny Tiny. All the children wanted to know where Freddy got him, and Freddy explained that he had borrowed him from Miss Pimm.

During the lunch period, Miss Coe put the little fellow on her desk and fed him his lunch. After lunch, the boys and girls drew pictures of Teeny Tiny sitting on his branch and then colored the pictures with wax crayons. Some of them made up stories about him.

Right after school, Mother, Freddy, and Linda started off in the car for Miss Pimm's with the hummingbird. As they rode along, Mother said, "Freddy, have you had a good time with Teeny Tiny in school today?"

"I surely have," said Freddy. "This little hummingbird was something very special."

CHAPTER 6:
EXCITEMENT AT THE WATERFALL

One day after school, Freddy was flying his toy airplane in the backyard when Linda came running up. "Oh, Freddy," she called. "Come right away! Flora and her ducks have gone over the waterfall!"

"Jiminy!" said Freddy. He and Linda ran as fast as they could go.

When Freddy and Linda got to the waterfall, they saw that the poor ducks were having a very bad time. The waterfall was beating down on them so fast that they could hardly keep above water. They were almost sinking.

"We must get help right away," said Freddy. "Linda, are your mother and father at home?"

"No," said Linda. "Mother has gone to Bradley Field to meet Daddy. Grandmother is taking care of me. She is sitting on the porch."

"Daddy is playing golf, and Mother has visitors for tea," said Freddy.

"Goodness me!" said Linda. "I am afraid the poor little ducks will drown."

"I think I know who could help us," said Freddy.

"Who?" said Linda excitedly.

"Mr. Donnelly," said Freddy. "He is the chief of the fire department. Sometimes he comes to our school to watch the fire drills. I'll go and telephone him."

"I'll stay here and holler for help," said Linda. "Perhaps someone will pass by and hear me."

Freddy ran across the road and into his house. Soon he came running back. "Oh, Linda," he called, "they are coming. I talked with Mr. Donnelly, and he said that he and two of his men would be right over."

"Good!" said Linda. "I hear the siren."

When the people in the houses nearby heard the siren, they came hurrying to see where the fire was. When they saw what was happening to the ducks, they said, "Oh, poor Flora! Oh, the darling little ducks! Someone should go right away and save them!" But no one did anything.

Soon Mr. Donnelly and the other two firemen drove up in Mr. Donnelly's red car. The two firemen in their hip boots and rubber coats and hats quickly waded into the madly gushing waterfall.

One of them, a big tall one, picked a baby duck up out of the water; and the other fireman, who was short and fat, picked up another. As soon as they caught a duck, they waded over close to the shore with it and handed it to the fire chief or to Linda or Freddy. The people who were watching cheered, and Tinker barked.

But Flora would not let anyone catch her until all eleven of her babies had been saved. Then the big tall fireman caught her and handed her to Mr. Donnelly.

When the fire chief put her down on the ground, she walked off quacking in a pleased voice, with her eleven happy babies following her, in a straight line, of course.

Flora led them to the shore of the pond, where they got into the water and swam up the stream.

Linda, Freddy, and the other people watched them until they disappeared from sight.

"Mr. Donnelly, I hope it was all right for us to call on you for help," said Freddy anxiously.

"Quite all right," said Mr. Donnelly. And his eyes twinkled.

"We are always glad to help in an emergency," said the tall fireman.

"Right you are!" said the short, fat fireman. Then he patted Tinker and said, "What a fine dog you have!"

"How do you like my kitten?" asked Linda, picking up Mixy and holding her in her arms.

Mr. Donnelly and the other firemen liked Mixy and said so.

"She's a calico kitten," said Linda.

"And I see she has double front paws," said Mr. Donnelly.

Mr. Donnelly patted Mixy and began naming her colors. "Orange, white, yellow, brown, black, gray, and tan," he said. "Seven colors and double front paws. You should take her to the cat show at the Children's Museum on Friday."

"I guess I will," said Linda. "What time is the show?"

"At four o'clock," said Mr. Donnelly. "I will look for you. I am to be a judge."

"What does it mean to be a judge?" asked Linda.

"The judges are the people chosen to decide which cats will be awarded the prizes," said Mr. Donnelly.

"I'll look for you," said Linda. "Watch

out for us."

"All right," said Mr. Donnelly. "Don't forget to come."

Then Mr. Donnelly and the other two firemen got into Mr. Donnelly's car and rode away.

The other people went back to their homes, and Linda and Freddy sat down on a bench on the shore of the pond and talked.

"It was a good thing you told me the ducks had gone over the waterfall," said Freddy.

"And it was a good thing that you called the fire department," said Linda.

Mixy climbed up into Linda's lap and

began to purr. "Oh, Mixy," said Linda, "I am going to take you to the cat show."

"I wish it were a pet show," said Freddy. "I should like to take Tinker. He would probably win a prize."

"I think Mixy will win one," said Linda.

"If Mixy wins a prize, what will it be for?" asked Freddy.

"For being so pretty and having such bright eyes," said Linda, hugging Mixy.

CHAPTER 7:
MIXY IN THE CAT SHOW

At three-thirty in the afternoon on the day of the cat show, Linda came over to ask Freddy to help her look for Mixy.

"Think of it, Freddy!" she said. "I can't find Mixy, and the show begins at four. I have been looking for her ever since I got home from school."

"Don't worry," said Freddy, "we will find her."

They looked in Linda's house and in the garage and on the terrace. In the house, they looked on every chair, on every table, on the sofa, on the beds, and under all the beds. They looked on the wide window sills in the living room and in the dining room. In the garage, they looked in the station wagon and under it. They looked on and under every chair on the terrace.

Then they went to the pond to see if she was sitting on the bench watching the ducks, or taking a nap in the sun.

Whenever they felt like giving up, Linda thought of one more place to look. They went from the pond back to Freddy's yard to look in Tinker's house. They called, "Come, Kitty, Kitty, Kitty! Come, Kitty, Kitty, Kitty!" But no Mixy came running to meet them.

At a quarter to four, Linda's mother came out to help look. In a few minutes, she said, "Linda, I think we should stop looking and go along to the show. You know we promised to pick up Janet and her kitten. We don't want them to be late."

Linda began to cry.

"Don't cry, Linda," said Freddy. "Probably there will be another cat show sometime, and you can take Mixy then."

Linda stopped crying. "Freddy, why don't you come with us?" she asked.

"I'd like to go," said Freddy, "but I am going to Farmington. Johnny Mills has invited me to see his new Shetland pony.

His father is coming for me at five."

As soon as Linda and her mother had gone, Freddy took his motorboat to the pond to play with it while he waited for Johnny's father to come.

But he did not feel like playing with the boat. He kept wondering where Mixy was. In a little while, he thought, "I'll take a walk to the top of the hill. Maybe the men who are working on the new house have seen her."

He put his motorboat down on the bench and hurried up the hill to the new house. But when he got close to the house, he found no workmen there. He tried the door. It was locked. "I'll go on to the other new house," he said to himself.

"Perhaps the men are working there."

Just as he started off, Freddy heard a faint meow. He stood still and listened. Soon he heard another meow. And another. Then he saw Mixy looking out at him from the picture window in the dining room. She was meowing.

"Oh, Mixy," called Freddy, "don't cry. I'll get you out."

He ran as fast as he could to the other new house. Mr. Davis, who was painting the house, knew Freddy. "Hello, my boy," he said. "Is there anything I can do for you?"

Freddy told him.

"I'll get the key and go along with you,"

said Mr. Davis.

When they got near the house, they saw Mixy still looking out of the window.

"Oh, ho!" said Mr. Davis. "That is the little kitten who was always underfoot here. She is pretty."

Mr. Davis opened the door, and Mixy met them in the hall. Freddy picked her up. Mr. Davis stroked her with his big hard fingers, and she began to purr.

Freddy thanked Mr. Davis and started home, thinking of the cat show. "Who will take Mixy?" he said to himself. "I can't take her. Johnny expects me. Perhaps Mother will know what to do." He hurried.

When he got to the house, he said to
Mother, "Here is Mixy. She was locked
in one of the new houses, and Mr. Davis
unlocked the door and let her out. But
who is going to take her to the show?"

"You might," said Mother. "You have
gone alone on the bus several times.
I would take you, but I am expecting
Grandmother and Grandfather for
supper."

"But, Mother," said Freddy, "this is
the day I go to Farmington to see Johnny
Mills' new pony."

Mother did not say anything. She gave
Mixy some milk in a saucer. Mixy lapped
it up with her little pink tongue.

"I suppose I could go to see Johnny

another time," said Freddy.

"I suppose you could," said Mother.

"If I went today, I might keep thinking about Mixy," said Freddy.

"That's right," said Mother.

Freddy thought over the problem for a minute or two more. Then he said, "I'll go to the show."

"Good for you!" said Mother. "I'll go get the bus fare."

Freddy telephoned to Johnny and told him about Mixy. Johnny invited him to come the next day.

When Freddy came back from the telephone, he found Mixy in a covered basket taking a nap. "I thought it might be easier to carry her in a basket," said Mother. She picked up the basket and said, "I'll go to the bus station with you."

Just as they got there, the bus came along. "When you get on, ask the driver to let you off at the Children's Museum," said Mother. She handed the basket to Freddy.

Freddy got on, paid his fare, and asked the driver to please let him off at the museum. Then he saw a friendly looking little old lady and sat down with her. "I like kittens," said the little old lady. "Put the basket on the seat between us."

Freddy did. Mixy woke up and sat up and looked about her. "What a pretty kitten!" said the little old lady. "I know

you take good care of her."

Freddy told her about Linda and the cat show.

"You will be glad you have taken her,"

said the little old lady. "It was the right thing to do."

Freddy smiled. "I think the show will be fun," he said.

Then the little old lady told him about her dog, and before Freddy knew it, the driver called out, "Children's Museum!" Freddy smiled at the little old lady and said goodbye.

He hurried from the bus and down the street a little way to the museum. A man at the door said, "Come this way," and led him into the big room where the show was being held. The room was filled with mothers and fathers and boys and girls. Freddy thought he had never before heard such a noise. People were talking and cats were meowing.

Freddy looked carefully about him, but he did not see Linda or her mother.

While he was wondering what to do next, a big boy came over to him and handed him a ticket with the number twenty-nine written on it. "When I call out your number, take the cat up to the judges' table," he said.

"But it isn't my cat," said Freddy. "This cat belongs to Linda Loomis."

"That's all right," said the boy. "Show her for Linda. What is the kitten's name?"

"Mixy," said Freddy.

The boy wrote Mixy's name on a card. "I have all the information I need," he said. "Listen for number twenty-nine." He grinned at Freddy and walked off.

Poor Freddy! He did not know what to do. But he walked up closer to the long table behind which the judges sat. Freddy did not know the women, but the man, sure enough, was Mr. Donnelly, the fire chief. He spied Freddy and winked. Freddy felt better.

He waited and waited. He listened carefully when the numbers were called and watched each owner put his cat down on the table. Finally, the man who was calling out the numbers said, "Number twenty-nine! Come right up, please!"

Freddy hurried to the table, still carrying Mixy in the basket. When he put the basket down, he heard someone call, "Oh, Freddy! You found Mixy!" And there was Linda standing beside him, nearly bursting with happiness.

Linda took Mixy from the basket and put her on the table. Then she stroked her and smiled at the judges.

One of the women said, "What a jolly-looking kitten!"

Mr. Donnelly said, "She has double front paws."

The other woman said, "She's a very mixed-up kitten! How many colors?"

"Seven," said Linda, and she quickly pointed them out.

When the judges had looked at all the

cats, they talked to each other, and then Mrs. Cheney, the head of the Children's Museum, awarded the prizes.

The prize for the best-looking Persian cat went to Princess, owned by Janet Brown. Princess was a black Persian with extraordinarily long silky fur. The prize was a book about taking care of pets.

Tommy Bevan's Siamese cat, Snubbins, won a prize. Snubbins had blue eyes and a glossy cream-colored coat, with face, ears, feet, and tail of chocolate brown. The prize was a narrow leather collar with a name plate fastened to it, and a tiny bell hung on the buckle.

"The third prize," said Mrs. Cheney, "goes to Bobsy, the only Manx cat at the show, owned by Timmy Watson." The prize was a rubber mouse that squeaked when it was pushed.

"The fourth prize," said Mrs. Cheney, "is this knitted catnip ball. It goes to Mixy, the cat with the mixed-up fur, owned by Linda Loomis."

Freddy thought of all the fun Mixy was going to have playing with the catnip ball.

CHAPTER 8:
DUSTY GOES VISITING

One day a present came in the mail for Freddy. It was a little clown hand puppet. He had a big nose for such a little fellow, and he had a huge grin on his face, and his little blue eyes looked sideways out of pink spectacle frames.

His clown's hat and jumper were shiny green, and on the front of his jumper were two big patches, one gold and one purple, and he wore lemon-colored gloves.

Freddy soon learned how to work the puppet. He would slip his hand into the puppet's jumper, put his thumb and little finger into each of the two arms, and get his other fingers into the puppet's head. By wiggling his fingers, he could make the puppet do all sorts of bows and turns and make all kinds of funny motions with his hands. And he could make him appear from inside the coat without anyone noticing that the puppet did not have any legs of his own but was really a hand puppet, with only a head and a body.

Freddy named the puppet Dusty. He thought that the most comical thing about him was his big plastic hands with the lemon-colored gloves that he could clap

together, or scratch his head with, or wave

hello or goodbye with when he felt like

it. Freddy liked the sharp little clicking

sound of Dusty's hands when he clapped

them together.

The very next day after Freddy got Dusty, he took him to school. When he told Miss Coe and the children the puppet's name, the boys and girls said, "Hello, Dusty!"

Dusty said hello to them in a squeaky little voice.

"Let's see if he knows how to add," said Miss Coe.

The boys and girls laughed. Then Linda said, "Dusty, how much are three and four?"

Dusty clapped his hands seven times.

Then the children asked Dusty how many eggs there are in a dozen, and then how many days there are in a week.

Dusty clapped the right number of times for each answer. But when they asked him how much five and three made, he clapped the wrong number of times.

Bobby Jones told him the right answer. "Thank you," said Dusty. "You are smarter than I am, Bobby."

"Bring Dusty in again next Friday," said Miss Coe. "And anyone else who has a puppet may bring him in then, too. They seem to go well with number work."

That day after school, Freddy said to Mother, "I wish Johnny Mills could see Dusty."

"Well," said Mother, "I am not busy this afternoon. We can take a run over to

Farmington to see him now."

"May we ask Linda to come with us?" said Freddy. "Linda has never seen Johnny's pony, and I know she would like to see him. Nipper is a very smart little pony."

"I think she might like to go along," said Mother. "Suppose you go and invite her."

In no time at all, Freddy came back with Linda. She had two lumps of sugar for Nipper.

"We will start right away," said Mother.

As they rode along, Freddy said, "Linda, when we get to Johnny's, let's look at Nipper first. Then I will show Dusty to Johnny. Dusty says that you are going to like Nipper, don't you, Dusty?"

Dusty nodded.

When they got to Johnny's house, they found Johnny, Nipper, and Johnny's big brother Jim all at home.

Linda gave Nipper one of the lumps of sugar, and of course he liked it. She stroked his beautiful black mane and said, "Nipper, you are a pretty pony! I wish I had you!"

Then Johnny said, "I'll saddle him, and you can ride him."

"But I am afraid," said Linda.

"You don't need to be," said Johnny. "Mary Minton, who lives next door, often rides him, and she is only five. She is not too little; Nipper is such a small pony."

"I want to see you ride, Freddy," said Linda. "Then maybe I will take a turn."

So Freddy got on Nipper, and Nipper started off. Freddy rode almost out of sight before he turned Nipper around and came back. He rode up to Mother and Linda, and Johnny called, "Now it is your turn, Linda."

Freddy slid down off Nipper, but Linda did not climb on.

"Nipper is really a gentle pony and easy to ride," said Johnny. "Only, never pull his reins too tight. He will run very fast if you do, and then stop short and slide you off."

"Dear me!" said Linda. "I wonder if I dare ride him."

"I think it will be safe enough," said Freddy's mother. "Just remember what Johnny says."

"All right," said Linda. "Show me how to hold the reins, Johnny. I will ride him on the grass. Then if I fall off, I won't get hurt too much."

Johnny laughed. "You are not going to fall off," he said. "Hang onto the saddle if you feel yourself slipping."

Linda climbed on Nipper, and Johnny showed her how to hold the reins. She

held them exactly right. Nipper gave her a
good ride.

When they got back, Linda slid down and gave Nipper the second lump of sugar.

After a while, Johnny and Freddy took off Nipper's saddle and put him in the pasture. And Johnny put up the three bars to the pasture gate. Then Freddy brought Dusty from the car to show him to Johnny.

"Dusty is good at number work," said Linda.

"Is he really?" asked Johnny.

"Try him and see," said Linda.

"Well, Dusty," said Johnny, "what number comes before thirty?"

"Twenty-nine," said a squeaky little

voice.

"Right!" said Johnny. "And what number follows forty-six?"

"Forty-seven," said the funny little voice, quick as a wink.

"Very good!" said Johnny. "Now, let's go and see my puppets. My brother Jim made them for me. I keep them in our cabin up on the hill behind the barn."

Mother wanted to go with them, so they all walked up the hill to the log cabin.

Jim had made a good many puppets for Johnny. Peter Rabbit, Curious George, and the peddler and the monkeys from Caps for Sale were all there.

While they were busy looking at the

puppets, Nipper came walking in. Mother and Freddy and Linda were surprised, of course, but not Johnny and Jim. They just said, "Hello, Nipper," and went on showing the puppets.

"How did he get out of the pasture?" asked Freddy.

"He has a trick," said Johnny. "He lifts out the middle bar and steps right over the bottom one."

"But what about the top bar? Does he knock it off, or does he raise it up?"

"Oh, he bends his knees a little and scrapes under it," said Johnny.

Then Johnny gave Nipper an apple. When the pony had finished eating it, he lay down at Johnny's feet like a great big dog and went to sleep.

Jim, Johnny, Mother, and Linda and Freddy went out of the cabin very quietly, so as not to wake Nipper.

Then Mother and Linda and Freddy said goodbye to Jim and Johnny and started for home.

CHAPTER 9:
GOODBYE, TEENY TINY

One Saturday morning in late September, Mother said, "Freddy, I have just made a chocolate cake. Uncle Ben likes chocolate cake. I could make plenty of sandwiches, and we could take Linda with us and have a picnic at Uncle Ben's."

"Let's," said Freddy. "And I wish we could call on Miss Pimm and see Teeny Tiny."

"Teeny Tiny may have already flown south," said Mother.

"I hope not," said Freddy. "I'd like to see him once more before he goes. And I should like to show Dusty to Uncle Ben."

Soon Mother and Freddy and Linda were riding along on their way to Uncle Ben's.

In a little while, they were on the outskirts of the town where they could see stretches of woods on both sides and away off on the hills. The trees were aglow with fall colors, and three or four leaves were coming down under every tree every minute.

"Look at all the pretty leaves," said Linda. "Red leaves and yellow leaves and orange leaves falling everywhere."

When they rode up to Uncle Ben's yard, he was up on a ladder picking apples. "Hello!" he called. "I'll be right down."

When he came down, Freddy showed Dusty to him.

When Uncle Ben heard about the picnic, he said, "I had an idea that I might have company today. I put several bottles of ginger ale in the icebox this morning."

Dusty said, "Oh, thank you!"

Then Linda said, "Watch him do his number work. Here's a good, hard example for him. Dusty, how much are six and three?"

Dusty clapped eight times.

"Wrong," said Linda. "Try again."

Uncle Ben quickly took a handful of pennies from his pocket and counted out six of them on the palm of his hand. "There they are," he said. "Six of them. Now I will add three more." And he counted out three more pennies. The palm of his hand was almost covered with pennies.

Then Uncle Ben took one of the pennies out of his hand and showed it to Dusty, and then closed his hand. "Now how many are left?" he asked.

Dusty clapped his hands together eight times.

"Right this time," said Linda.

"Uncle Ben, have you seen Miss Pimm

lately?" asked Freddy.

"Yes," said Uncle Ben. "I saw her yesterday at Mr. Norton's store."

"Did she say anything about the hummingbird?" asked Freddy.

"No," said Uncle Ben. "I forgot to ask about him. Perhaps he has already left for the south."

"I wonder if he has," said Freddy. "I wish we could see him."

"We will go to see Miss Pimm in a little while," said Uncle Ben. "But don't be too disappointed if you find that he has gone. Many birds have already gone. The chilly nights at this time of year make them wish for a warmer climate. They are almost all gone by Halloween every year—all except the sparrows, the starlings, the chickadees, and the other birds that stay here all winter."

"Where do the hummingbirds go?" Freddy asked.

"To Mexico and Central America," said Uncle Ben.

Then Uncle Ben suggested that they take a walk to the lake. They walked through the apple orchard and the huckleberry bushes to the lake. Linda and Freddy went in wading. The water was cold, but the sun was hot. A raft had been pulled up close to the dock. Linda and Freddie sat on the raft in the sunshine, splashing their feet in the chilly, quiet water.

Then Uncle Ben said, "Wouldn't this be a good time to call on Miss Pimm? I'll be glad to row us over, and perhaps Freddy will row us back."

"Right you are!" said Freddy.

They got into the boat, and Uncle Ben rowed along in the warm September sunshine to Miss Pimm's dock.

Miss Pimm came down from her garden to the dock to meet them. "Won't you get out and visit with me?" she asked. "I believe I have enough chairs on the lawn, but if not, we will fetch some from the porch."

"Let's ask Dusty how many more we

shall need," said Linda. "Freddy, show Dusty to Miss Pimm."

Freddy did, and Linda said, "Dusty, how many more chairs do we need?"

Dusty shook his head and did not clap at all.

"He knows there are just enough," said Freddy. "He is going to sit with me."

"Goodness me!" said Miss Pimm.

They went and sat down.

"Is Teeny Tiny still here?" asked Freddy.

"I believe he is," said Miss Pimm. "Not right here in the yard, but somewhere nearby. Every morning now when he flies off, I wonder if I shall ever see him again. I expect him to leave any day now for the south."

"Does he still sleep in his strawberry basket at night?" asked Linda.

"Yes," said Miss Pimm. "During the day I keep the basket on the table on the porch. At bedtime I always find him in it and bring it into the house."

"That's good," said Linda. "He is pretty small to be outdoors after dark."

"My brother visited me last week," said Miss Pimm. "I told him that I was afraid Teeny Tiny might not be getting enough to eat, especially since the blossoms have all gone. He rigged up the arrangement you see there."

Miss Pimm pointed to a bottle hanging on a pole. The pole was fastened to the side of the house. "I always keep either honey and water or honey and milk in the bottle," she said. "This morning I put in honey and milk. I think Teeny Tiny prefers it."

Just as she finished speaking, Linda said in a soft, excited voice, "Oh, look! There he is!"

Everyone looked, and there, sure enough, was Teeny Tiny, moving his wings so fast that all they could see was a little fuzzy blur on each side of him while he took a drink. He made a fine loud humming sound.

Freddy and Linda walked up close and listened.

"He stands still like a helicopter," said Freddy. "And he hums like one, too."

When he had finished drinking, Teeny Tiny flew away. He disappeared as if by magic.

"I am glad his wing is all better," said Freddy. "Now he can fly all the way to Central America if he needs to."

"He flies very fast," said Linda. "He went like lightning."

"Will it take him long to get to his winter home?" asked Freddy.

"It will take him a good many days," said Miss Pimm.

"Goodness me!" said Linda. "Do the robins and all the other birds fly that far when they go away for the winter?"

"I believe so," said Miss Pimm.

"The same robin came back to our yard this spring and built his nest again in our apple tree," said Freddy.

"Birds often come back to the same place," said Miss Pimm. "I hope Teeny Tiny comes back here."

In a few minutes, they said goodbye to Miss Pimm, and Freddy rowed them back to Uncle Ben's dock. Then they went to his yard, sat on the grass, and ate the sandwiches and the chocolate cake and drank the ginger ale out of his icebox. Uncle Ben said that the chocolate cake was the best he had ever eaten. And Mother and Linda and Freddy said that the ginger ale was just right.

When it was time to go, Uncle Ben gave them a basket of apples and said, "Don't be like the birds and migrate for the winter."

"Why, Uncle Ben," said Freddy. "Halloween is coming soon. I always come to see you on Halloween in my costume."

"That's right," said Uncle Ben. "Be sure to bring Linda with you this time."

"You will never guess who I am," said Linda. "Freddy will probably bring Dusty

with him, and that will give him away.
But I know you will never recognize me."

"I think I will leave Dusty at home on
Halloween," said Freddy. "I don't want
him to see any witches."

Then Mother, Linda, and Freddy said
goodbye to Uncle Ben.

On the way home, Linda said, "Freddy,
I like all your friends."

"And they all like you, too," said
Freddy.

THE END